Copyright © 2014 by Emmanuel Ngwainmbi
Cover illustration by David Dodd
Design by Aaron Rosenberg
ISBN 978-1-941408-13-1 — ISBN 978-1-941408-14-8 (pbk.)
All rights reserved. No part of this book may be used or reproduced in any manner whatsoever without written permission except in the case of brief quotations embodied in critical articles and reviews.
For information address Crossroad Press at 141 Brayden Dr., Hertford, NC 27944
www.crossroadpress.com

First edition

Bo Aku, Undisputed King of the Forest

EMMANUEL NGWAINMBI

Acknowledgment

The author wishes to thank the principals, teachers, students, and high schools in Bavaria, Germany for organizing workshops and taking part in his lectures on these stories, and Ariah Miller and the students at Elizabeth City Middle School for producing some of the drawings based on their understanding of the stories.

About the Book

Bo Aku, Undisputed King of the Forest and Other Stories is an adaptation of some sixty myths and legends collected in Africa with a research grant from the Southern Education Foundation.

The stories describe the experiences of children and parents confronted by a gorilla and lion in the African jungle. They are eclectic, rich in moral values, humorous, suspenseful, and contain wisdom. They seek to enlighten the reader about Bantu African mythology and other ways of reasoning. They open the door to an enchanted universe where the child learns that every evil phantom has its opposite that is more powerful and worth imitating.

The legends and folktales are set against the backdrop of Bantu culture, steeped in mysticism and logical reasoning that date back to the 12th century A.D., when interdependent villages existed in the grasslands and mountains of the black tribes in the Benue and Adamawa regions, a part of what is known today as West Africa. Chad, Gabon, Nigeria, Benin, Senegal, Ivory Coast, and Mali are among the twenty-two countries in northwest Africa.

The Kingdom of Kom, situated in the northwestern Africa, has a diverse and rich culture. Events, dates, and artifacts bear special meaning to the people.

Story telling is a centuries-old family-oriented educational experience. For the African family, it is like watching a movie with great suspense on a family channel.

Whether they have been invited or not, strangers from the neighborhood pick a home they want to visit. They arrive early in the evening and chit-chat with the family members until dinner is served. After dinner, the older people tell folktales to lure children to sleep. Parents ask their children to put out the fire in the hearth and get into their beds and close their eyes. Their parents and older people would then begin to tell tales. Some children would quickly fall asleep.

When reading this aloud, it is suggested that the narrator use humor and good voice management skills to sustain the audience's concentration until the end. Like the main actor in a movie, the narrator must be able to use stunts, engage the audience in the action, sing, raise, or drop his voice according to the pace of the character's action. The narrator must imitate their sounds and actions, to convince the audience that he is in fact the animal. Ninety-nine percent of the heroes and villains in the stories are animals.

The narrator starts with a question: *"Mogana?"* ("May I tell a story?"), and the listeners reply, *"Sun ngayn,"* ("Yes, you may"). From the response, the narrator knows who is still awake. The call-and-response approach suggests not only the participatory experience between the storyteller and listeners, but, most importantly, it engages both parties in a educational activities wherein the keen listener prompts, redirects, or corrects the teller when he omits a section or uses a term not known to the audience.

The stories should be informative reading for 5th to 7th grade students and to people interested in adventure.

Table of Contents

Chapter One: Bah, the Inquisitive Messenger
Chapter Two: Bo Aku, King of the Forest
Chapter Three: The Boys Go on a Dangerous Adventure
Chapter Four: Rooster Takes on the Lion
Chapter Five: Children Guard a Farm
Chapter Six: Marta Turns Detective on Her Farm
Chapter Seven: The Greedy King Meets his Fate
Chapter Eight: Fame and her daughters in the Jungle
Chapter Nine: Bo Aku Meets the Villagers
Chapter Ten: The Villagers Engage Bo Aku
Chapter Eleven: Bo Aku and the Villagers Reach a Deal

Chapter One
Bah, the Inquisitive Messenger

They thought the world was coming to an end as the wind howled through the villages. Stunned villagers stayed inside their huts clinging to each other. Only Bah's father was outside, partially shielded by the huts on the banks of the Menchum Waterfall. He shivered with fear and ducked, protecting his face with his hands as the wind tore countless leaves from the trees in the thick forest. Debris quickly piled up on everything around him. Twigs slapped his tiny frame as they flew about carelessly, forcing him to wince and lament.

With the roof pounding constantly, people thought of large animals walking ten feet tall, crushing dry leaves and twigs as they roamed the wilderness. Doors remained shut. Moisture hung in the air like tendrils from a thick soup. Taking a deep breath was like swallowing warm, salty water. The sky was black, even as the sun pushed waves of heat throughout the village. Bah's father thought he would die any moment as he murmured to himself, "I'm not going down without a fight." Then he heard a voice whispering, "You are still here, fight!"

But all of them were more afraid of Bo Aku, the tallest, strongest, fastest gorilla in the rainforest than other wild animals.

Later, children trembled as they opened their doors to visit neighbors. None of them dared ask to go out alone. Mother always walked with her children, and no sister or brother was ever left alone in the hut.

Brothers Banga, Mani and Bah their friend stayed inside. Milla and Song Bah's cousins, also best of friends with the other three boys, watched with studious eyes as the wind ravaged the stormed through the green pastures tearing off branches and dismembering plants.

Bo Aku often destroyed the vegetation by trampling on grass and fighting with deer, polar bears, and chimpanzees. For no particular reason, he broke tree branches when he got angry. He showered in Menchum Waterfall, the largest waterfall in the Grasslands of the northwestern region of Cameroon, and basked in the sun, stretching out his large body and long legs over the thicket, fully confident no one would ever threaten his space, the entire forest, the waterfall and the surrounding farmlands.

For as long as eleven-year-old Bah could remember, his father had been the brave one, planting food for the village. Who else would have the courage to travel along the swollen river to the fields where the vegetables grew? It was only after the rain stopped and the skies grew blue again that Bah could leave the village to work with his father, cultivating and harvesting okra, pumpkins, and cocoyam.

"You must be careful under the rain. Bo Aku waits for you to wander away from your hut. Then he grabs you. You'll never be seen again," his mother said as she prepared the evening meal.

Throughout their lives, the children had heard horrid stories about Bo Aku, the gorilla who reigned in the dense forest. Farmers and hunters made sure they returned home before dusk. Around dusk, Bo Aku blocked the footpath, and shepherded unsuspecting ones to his home deep in the forest where he made them his slaves. The obedient ones became his children and he ate the stubborn, clever ones. Everyone was scared of him; some tired of leaving their chores unfinished to rush back home just to avoid being kidnapped. The village soldiers had tried to kill Bo Aku one night, but Bo Aku's soldiers captured them and made them slaves. So the entire village was frustrated. Even the king of the village had never set up a scheme to kidnap Bo Aku. Some of the friends of the children who lived in the village were among Bo Aku's captives.

Bah had spent sleepless nights wondering why one animal terrorized everyone and got away with it. Whenever he heard a new story about Bo Aku, he felt angrier. The boys felt the same way and talked more among themselves about meeting him. They were in awe about his superpowers and wanted to meet him. Perhaps seeing him in his own neighborhood might give them an idea of what could make him vulnerable. Bah cooked up a plan and decided to share it. He visited the boys in their homes and called a meeting and pleaded with their parents to allow them to meet.

One evening after finishing their chores, the children had gathered at the center of the village playground. Bah told them it would be dangerous if all of them entered into Bo Aku's premises at once. He asked each child to observe and study Bo Aku's lifestyle and report findings at their next meeting. Some were to observe the times he left his house and went to the forest. Bill was assigned to take note of the moments he ordered people to work, when he might take a nap, and when he might go foraging for food.

They all agreed and returned home determined not to inform anyone of their plan.

The next spring, Bah and his friends held a ceremony in honor of Eto and Bill who had disappeared mysteriously on a dark and rainy morning. Bah carved masks out of zebrawood and painted them to look just like the missing friends. He built a small raft and placed the masks on the raft. Then he sent it spinning down the river on its journey into the ever-mysterious dark rainforest that stood in the horizon.

He was still scared of the stories he had heard about wild animals and ghosts always fighting in the rainforest.

Not this time! His friends could be under the grip of Bo Aku, dying.

"May the masks protect our friends and bring them back to us," Bah said with his head bowed. Surely he would never see them again.

Bah's parents worked the farm that was farthest from the village. When it was too late to return to the village, small huts along the way provided protection. Staying overnight was always something Bah looked forward to, even though he heard strange animal noises and winds whispering for him.

"Go home, Bah, go home! It is safer in your own home."

Sounds kept him awake until Mother or Father would tell tales of brave animals and brave children. Bah always wondered if he was brave. Would he know what to do if Bo Aku charged out of the forest? They would soon find out.

Early one morning, Mother woke Bah and said, "We have to go to the farm. Your father needs help harvesting the yams." Bah thought, *I get to lead my friends on a trip to the farm and help Father with the harvest. He must think I am very brave and smart!*

Bah told his mother, "I'm sure they can come. I will help them when their fathers need help."

The bright, red sun smiled down on the five children as they followed Bah's mother along the calm river. Pleased with their journey, the children nodded back at the sun. They could hear the crunch of their feet on the sandy bank. They kept looking at the zebrawood trees that looked like tall warriors guarding Bo Aku's forest.

They followed a curve around the river and found Bah's father standing among the rows of tall, snaky yam shrubs supported by sticks. He smiled at them and waved.

"Father, we're here to help you harvest!" Bah yelled as he ran through the first leafy yam bushes.

"We will work until just before the sundown. Then we will have a meal and tell stories. Would you like that?" Bah's father asked.

The three boys quickly agreed. Then they raised their hands and asked, "Where do we start?"

The twin girls, dressed alike in brightly colored dresses, their hair tightly curled in matching rows, asked in unison, "Can we help prepare the meal?"

"Yes, come with me, and we can start the meal now," Bah's mother responded.

As they went about their tasks, the children did not notice the slight movement between two of the tallest zebrawood trees.

The boys went into the rows of yam shrubs and started turning over the dirt. "The weeds gobble up the nourishment and keep the yams from growing," Bah's father told them. "It is most important for the yams to get all the nourishment. Do not miss any of those weeds!"

It was hard work, bending over in the sun and making sure that the roots of the weeds were returned to the soil. After a few hours, Bah's father noticed that the boys were slowing down. "We are almost finished. Look up and see the sun. We have to stop before it reaches the tops of the trees," he said.

Then he added, "Who wants to help get the fire started?"

"I do, Father," Bah, said pushing his tiny body in front of Mani and Banga, eager to show his father his enthusiasm.

"I'll finish the row," Bah's father said, nodding his approval.

The boys picked up their tools and marched back to the hut, complaining about aches and pains from a long day in the field.

"Look at these blisters on my hands. They hurt when I touch them," Banga said.

"My back hurts just above my hip," Mani said, pretending to limp.

"My shoulders feel very tight," Bah said as he punched Mani in the hip.

Bah's mother was standing outside the hut when they arrived. "It is good your father sent you home early. Bah, please take this bucket. I need you to go to the hut around the bend in the river. Can you see the smoke? That is Bella's hut. She will give you hot coals. We need them to start the fire."

Bah set off for the hut. As he turned toward the smoke, he wondered if his mother had been right about who owned the hut. The door looked larger than Bella and her family needed. The entire hut looked newer and grander than he had imagined. As he approached it, he overheard moaning nearby, tilted his ear and inched closer, looking furtively around to make sure no one was watching. The sounds grew louder and louder. He looked inside the dark hut. Then he sauntered to the back of the hut. He could not believe what was unfolding before his eyes.

He opened his mouth and his eyes rolled with surprise. "Eto, Bill!" he cried out. What are you doing here? Everyone has been looking for you." They looked up with wet, red eyes, leaves wrapped around their mouth and hands tied behind their back. Mariel frantically turned her head to the left trying to point to something moving some fifty yards away. It was Bo Aku.

"Get up," Bah said feverishly, lifting Bill up. He untied his hands and removed the leaves from his mouth; Billy then untied Mariel's hands and they scurried off, glancing back to make sure Bo Aku had not spotted them.

Bo Aku slapped the thicket with his palm as he drifted toward them, groaning ever so loudly. "Stop! I told you to stay there," he shouted, "Stop if you want to stay alive!"

Bah scurried around the hut and picked the path leading to the village. Mariel and Billy followed, keeping a keen eye on Bo Aku's speed as he stumped toward them with an angry look, growling.

Chapter Two
Bo Aku, King of the Forest

Bo Aku sat inside the left corner of his new hut, gracefully watching the river rumble down toward the ocean. Flanked by tall, dark iroko trees and thick grass, River Koinu was feared more than Bo Aku. Children who went there to swim or wash their clothes without letting their parents come along drowned. Their bodies were later found floating on the shores, badly decomposed. The villagers believed the sea goddess had drowned them and had taken their souls to the bottom of the river to help her with her chores. They never returned to the village.

Bo Aku had many dwelling sites scattered all over the forest built by the parents and children he had once kidnapped. The hut was like a cave. It was a tall with no windows and made of brown clay. The door was thatched with banana leaves and Indian bamboo and plastered with mud. He could pick any hut to relax in, but the hut near the river was his favorite spot. Children, men, and women used a footpath nearby to get to the river to wash their food crops.

Bo Aku arched forward and looked curiously when something moved. He had trained his ears, and he could separate the footsteps of the children from those of animals. The children moved forward stealthily while animals stumped about noisily crushing twigs and leaves and dismantling shrubs.

When a fight broke out, the animals ran wild, taming the bushes. They scuffled and wrestled each other to the ground, mother against mother, child against child, and so on, and left behind splatters of blood and beaten-down grass when the fight was over. Bo Aku would only stand back and watch the scuffle from a safe distance. Often, he just walked away.

The smoke from the fire twirled into the sky; a signal he knew would attract one of the children. He had seen them as he stood tall and silent between the zebrawood trees. *Just a few more*, he thought. *Just a few more, and my own family will be complete.*

He was eight feet tall, with round, sad eyes. He only had to think of his childhood as a baby gorilla to feel afraid and alone.

On a cool night, five-year-old Bo hid among leaves in the tallest tree.

He watched as a strange smoke hit his own mother, father, and five brothers and sisters. The smoke pushed them to the ground.

The hunters wrapped each member of his family in a bag. They took the two big bags and threw them in the river and took away smaller bags, each containing a gorilla child, as silently as the night had begun.

Bo never saw his parents or brothers and sisters again. He grew up protected by the elephants and hippos that had learned how to avoid the hunters.

"Bo Aku will never fear the hunters again. He will be the biggest gorilla in the forest. He has nothing to fear," the elephant predicted.

"I see him with tears in his eyes, even though he is already the biggest, fastest, and strongest adult in the rainforest. I think he may be missing his family," the hippo said.

"Don't be fooled by the tears," elephant replied. "He may be shedding crocodile tears. Wait until he gets hungry."

"He would feed on fruits, his principal diet, and on leaves, buds and blossoms. So I am not worried about my own life," replied the hippo.

"When hooting, screaming, grunting, and drumming starts on those hollow spots in the trees with the flat of his hands, you don't want to be around there."

"You seem to know him so well," the hippo said, nodding with approval. "Do you spend a lot time with him?"

"I know his family. His wife spends years nursing and caring for her infant before giving birth again. Sometimes I hang around him for hours, but not when he starts skipping from tree to tree. The noise he makes while skipping and slapping things annoys me. So I walk away," elephant said, looking sad. "He is worse than the leopard and the human being. He throws large sticks at his enemies."

"I can see that you know that family very well," the hippo said.

"Of course I do. You know I take my time to walk around this forest, to see who is doing what, where, how, and when and with whom," elephant boasted, waving its tusks. "Chimps make specific calls when they need food and are in danger, and each chimp has a unique hoot that distinguishes it from the others. They like to communicate non-verbally, just like humans. They use facial expressions a lot to show their feelings. But you don't want to hang around when chimps are hungry or scared." He mimicked the sound and tried to move his huge body to demonstrate.

The hippo laughed.

"It is not funny. I have seen them overcome their enemies. Their most frequent victims are young baboons, colobus monkeys, and blue monkeys."

Bo still feared the hunters. They might come back for him some day. He longed for his own family to protect him. But they knew they could not allow themselves to be lured into his den. Though he was often noisy, he was also curious, intelligent, and social.

He became the enemy of any animal that tried to cross his path. He had a thickset body with long arms, short legs, and no tail. His body was covered with long black hair, but his face, ears, fingers, and toes were bare. His red eyebrows, lips, and earlobes made it easy for hunters to find him. His long hands could grip anything firmly and allow him to pick up any object. So the animals avoided Bo as he ruled his part of the forest. Even the small reptiles and insects eventually left his forest. When he was bored, Bo would hoot and scream at the top of his voice and saunter about the place and hop from tree to tree in search of a companion.

Bo had two boys hidden so deep in the forest that no one would ever find them. If he had three more boys and two more girls, he would have his family back. Nobody would dare take them away. They would stay with him forever.

He waited.

The boys walked up to the door and stealthily knocked.

"What can I do for you?" Bo asked, standing up.

They just stared and said nothing.

"Uh, uh, where is Mrs. Bella?" He asked, looking over their heads.

"Are you Bo Aku?" Bah asked, walking backwards. Bo reached out to take the bucket and instead swept the boy off his feet and dropped him in a bag as Banga fled. He took the bag to the back of the hut and hung it against a branch of a large zebrawood tree.

Bo returned to the side of the hut, chanting and hopping with excitement. *Three now, three under my roof.* He halted and wondered if more could be on the way there. And what would he do with these captured children? He thought to himself, *I could start a new family and form many generations of my clan. They cannot replace my own family. Perhaps I should just wait. If other children come this way, I will put them away and force the villagers to find my family before I can release their children. If no else comes here, what will I do with them? I do not have enough food to raise them. I do not even have the time to look after them.*

He started to go toward the bags to release the children when a thought crossed his mind: he might never see his own family again. He returned to his hut, expecting their parents to come to him and make an offer.

The wind howled, tossing leaves and dry twigs into the air. Roofs crackled and split into pieces and trees swayed mercilessly in one direction from the fifty-mile-per-hour wind. Everyone stayed inside waiting. Some were on their knees praying, others looked hopelessly outside through cracks on the walls. The storm was relentless as hell stones rained on everything below the sky, punching holes in the ground, quickly piling up hailstones on the grass, furrows, and playgrounds.

Chapter Three
The Boys Go on a Dangerous Adventure

Banga shivered under the shade, glancing fearfully from left to right to see if Bo Aku was coming. His hand still gripped the branch, but he was not sure how much longer he would be holding it or what he might do if the monster startled him. Bo Aku knew every corner of the forest; he owned it.

Mrs. Bella, Banga's mother, Mariel and other villagers had not seen the children, and grew more worried. The playground had been deserted. Other children, fearing Bo Aku might visit the playground and take them away, stayed at home. Men, women and children quickly gathered in each other's homes and discussed plans to find the children and the parents. They knew Banga and Bah Mani had gone to the farm to watch the birds. If they were not watching birds, they were hunting animals for dinner or playing. They had not returned to the village. Could Bo Aku be back at his game, snatching people away? They were not so sure.

So they went to find out from Bomufuh, the native doctor. The big-bellied, bald, gray-headed father of twenty-five children could look among his magic things and say for sure where they were. His homestead was located near a cave six kilometers away from the village. Thankfully, the cave was on the opposite side of the forest, safe from the trappings of Bo Aku. It had a barb-wired fence so high a boy could not see the green banana leaves and coffee trees unless he entered the compound. The double door was secured with a big lock made of mahogany wood. Any visitor who arrived at the gate shouted and announced his name and those of his ancestors before they could be allowed inside Bomufuh's compound.

Still the villagers would not take any chances. They had machetes and they walked in single file. The person in front often threw rocks into the forest to fool Bo Aku or lure him to a tight space while they hastened through the place the rock had dropped. The hyenas and cobs were not to be ignored, either. They could smell human flesh from a distance. So they lowered their bodies to avoid detection and walked gingerly, halting whenever something moved.

When they arrived at Bomufuh's compound, they found him sitting on an old stool in the yard, just in front of his hut. The compound had twelve huts built around a fig tree. The huts belonged to Bomufuh's wives, children and cousins, but the forty inhabitants were not home. They were in their various farms and in the bush, expected back in the evening. Behind the huts were the coffee and banana farms and vegetable gardens. On the far end stood a small grassy hut where Bomufuh's jujus and ancestral spirits lodged. Everyone knew their role was to protect the entire village from evil people and soldiers from neighboring villages. No wonder the women and men did not come there too often.

"I knew you were coming," he said, looking at them one by one as they filed up. "Welcome, please have a seat." He said showing them empty stools next to dry animal skulls and seashells spread across the floor. They obeyed.

Bomufuh gathered the shells in his hands and raised them toward his lips. He whispered a few words, raised his hand above his head, and splashed the things across the floor. He leaned forward, casting a keen eye at the shells. "Aih, aih, aih, I thought so!" he exclaimed. He sat upright, tilted his head to the right side and said, "Your children are stowed away in a bag over there." He pointed to the forest. "They are in a lot of trouble. The dreaded gorilla has them. He could eat them at any moment."

"We cannot fight him. What should we do now?" Bella asked, shaking with fear and anger.

"Wait," the doctor replied, gathering the things again. He shook them, flung them on the floor and studied them one by one. He picked them up with his left hand. "These strangers here want to know what to do. They want their children back. Give me an answer now." He spoke to the things inside his hands, paused and dropped them back on the floor. Then he dropped them on the floor and flipped each piece over and back again with his fingers.

They watched his face, hoping to detect meaning.

"Wow," he exclaimed. "This one is above me! Bo Aku is furious. Two boys have upset him, boys from your village. He has kidnapped one of them; the other one is still in the forest. He is hiding in a tree. I see him in a shade, but he will not be staying there for long. Bo Aku is looking for him. If he finds the boy he will break his bones."

"We will find him," Mrs. Bella said. They thanked Bomufuh and stormed away.

"I don't think he's that smart," Mani's mother said as they headed for the smoke.

"There, over there! That is the hut! Bah is probably inside having a treat," Mrs. Bella exclaimed.

As Milla and Song watched Banga and Mani go after Bah, they both shook their heads in dismay. "Those two will never find Bah, we had best go ourselves," Milla said to Song.

"Let's go," Song replied. "We'll bring them all back and surprise Bah's mother!"

"There, that's the hut." Milla said.

"Something is wrong. I just know it," Bah's mother, Mrs. Tall, said as she approached the door of the hut.

She was wondering what had happened to her five little helpers. "My husband will be home soon, I'd best go myself and find the children," Mrs. Tall said.

She was starting to worry as she walked the entire distance from the village to the farm—three kilometers. She knew the stories of Bo Aku. It was her responsibility to get the children back before her husband returned from the fields. He had reminded her to keep an eye on the children while he was away for they were quite daring.

She knew there was a problem as she came closer to the hut with the large door. The door itself was much too large, even for Mrs. Bella and her family. Bah's mother walked around to the back of the hut and saw five bags hanging from the limbs of a large zebrawood tree.

Her eyes opened wide and she was crying as she moved closer to the bags. Hands and feet were silhouetted against the sides.

"Bah, Mani, Banga, are you in those bags?

"Mother, Mother, hurry! He will be back soon. He says he needs a wagon. We don't know why," Bah whispered.

As she reached out to Bah's bag, Bo Aku landed next to her. "They are mine now," he said. He picked up Bah's mother, threw her into a bag, and hung it next to the children.

Bah's mother heard Bo Aku say, "Now I need another wagon, there are just too many."

Just at that moment, there was silence. An old forest elephant walked by the bags. She lifted her trunk and sniffed at the first bag. Bah's mother recognized the sound of her large feet and called out to her. "Please help us. We will return the favor."

"Who put you there?" the elephant asked.

"Bo Aku. Surely you are not afraid of him! You're so much bigger!" Bah's mother said.

"I wish I could help you. But I raised Bo Aku after his family was stolen. I cannot do anything to cause him pain," the elephant said, walking away.

Then a hippo came out of the river. She shook her body off, spraying the bags. "Please help us! We will return the favor someday," Bah's mother cried out as she peeped through a small hole in the bag.

"Who put you there?" the hippo asked.

"Bo Aku. Surely you are not afraid of him! You're so much bigger!"

"I wish I could help you. But I took care of Bo Aku after his family was taken away. I cannot do anything to cause him pain," responded the hippo as she walked away.

A tortoise shuffled up to Bah's bag.

Bah looked down and said, "Oh, please help us. We will return the favor someday."

But the tortoise shrugged and walked away, murmuring, "What can I do? I am just a tortoise."

As the tortoise disappeared into the forest, a large rooster came running up to the zebrawood tree. "I am not afraid of that big baboon. He is nothing to me," he shouted, flying up to untie the bags. "I will get my team together and defeat him if I have to", he vowed, lifting his feet toward the ropes. Then he carefully untied the bags.

The captives jumped out and started adjusting their clothes, hugging each other.

"Thank you for letting us out. We will repay you," Bah's mother said, giving him a big hug as her heart thumped along.

The Rooster quietly led them behind a huge tree in his home as they walked rather stealthily looking suspiciously to their left and their right. He told them to stay there and remain quiet.

"Wait a minute. I'll be right back" Bah said. Hee scurried into the hut and returned with a bucket of hot coals for their own fire at home.

"Father must be getting hungry. Let's go!"

The moment the captives left, the Rooster rushed back to the neighborhood and discussed how they would face Bo Aku if he decided to attack them. They agreed to stage a performance to distract him. Each animal had skills.

Bo returned and found six empty bags and four sets of animal tracks. He thought someone had come to let the children out, but he did not know who.

He did know the prints of the elephant and the hippo. He knew that they were his friends. He also knew that the tortoise prints belonged to an animal too slow and too awkward to have untied the bags because they were everywhere. So he went looking for the rooster. The Rooster was well known throughout the region for mischief. He knew how to convince friends to fight against each other while he mused at their foolish actions. He then presented himself as judge and brought peace among them after they had exhausted their energy. He would have the loser of the fight shake hands with the winner and then he would take them out to dinner and a concert. He would organize a concert for smaller birds and animals in their neighborhood, making sure they were not too loud. For the sounds could attract the lions and tigers there. Then, he would make them guests of honor and have them pay a fee to get into a concert featuring Mother Hen and her five chicks. Other members of the audience were the gorilla, lion, wasp, spider, bee, the children from the village and their families. The funnier the entertainment, the higher was the entrance fee.

The most expensive entertainment he set up involved Mother Hen scrambling for grains of corn with her chicks. Before the drama started, he asked the audience to select a winner—Mother Hen or the chicks—but he never told them the duration of the game. He did not reveal the price the winner would get, either. Once the birds had swallowed all the corn, he drove them away and declared the entire contest over. He told them, based on the sudden end of the game, that no one had won, so he had to keep the prize for himself.

Bo Aku found the rooster sitting on a fence in front of his own home, carefully trimming his toenails. He had no idea the Rooster had brought along his friends to begin negotiations for peace in the region. The Spider , Mosquito and Bee were lurking in a dark corner, buzzing quietly and determined not be seen.

Bo Aku hid behind a tree and thought of the best way to approach Rooster and make him reveal the whereabouts of the children. Killing the Rooster would be the worst thing, he thought. Suddenly a strange feeling gripped his soul; the children might not be alive. He wanted them returned to him safe and healthy. He did not wish to frighten him—the Rooster could escape by flying into the woods and keep changing his home.

He shook a tree branch and laughed hysterically. The Rooster turned his head sharply, frightened by his voice.

"Stay calm. I will not hurt you," Bo Aku said and slowly appeared, advancing toward the Rooster. "You know why I am here."

The Rooster was still not sure of what he had just heard. He tilted his ear to the right, imagining the gorilla's hands squeezing his neck as he came closer, his large feet trampling on twigs. He thought of his big eyes, huge lips, and clenched teeth while he strangled him. The Rooster moved his head to the left, wondering what he would do to avoid instant death. He felt it would be useless to jump down and peck Bo Aku's body—the pain would be insignificant to the gorilla. It might be best to distract him with a joke, he thought, tilting his head. As Bo Aku stretched out his long arm toward him, the Rooster flapped his wings as a sign of warm welcome. Then he smiled and replied, "Yes, I know. You have come to have dinner with your friend."

Bo Aku looked stunned by the response. He halted and asked the Rooster if he was expecting a friend. The Rooster jumped down and slowly walked toward him with a smile, pointing at his chest. "You. Only friends visit friends."

"I understand that, but this is no time for parties. My children are missing," Bo Aku hollered.

Rooster's beak twitched. He stepped backwards and flapped his wings again, thinking of what to say. His friends Wasp, Spider, Scorpion, Grasshopper and Bee were in his house listening. He decided he needed to ask his friends for help and thought of calling them out. But calling them out could force Bo Aku to attack him. Bo Aku himself might be wary of being attacked. He might launch his own assault first. Wrong idea! Moreover, Rooster felt that since Bo Aku had traveled all day to meet him, he must have suspected Rooster might know something about the children's disappearance. No other animal in the entire forest had ever dared to touch whatever belonged to him.

He moved his beak toward his ribs pretending to scratch it, but his eyes searched over the fence for something to distract Bo Aku. There were bunches of ripe bananas, pineapples, and palm nuts. He asked Bo Aku to go feast on them. "This is your home. Make yourself comfortable," he added.

Bo Aku's throat moved with excitement when he saw the bananas. He quickly stretched his hairy arm over the fence, keeping another eye on Rooster to make sure he would not escape. Rooster sneaked inside and told the animals the rest of the story, expecting a quick solution.

"We have a huge problem on our hands," cried Wasp.

The Spider wondered who in his right mind would negotiate anything with a gorilla, the King of the Forest. He argued that bees have influence, too, and told the group to attack the gorilla. Bees could drone in his ears and distort his mind. Spider suggested a form of entertainment to put him in a jovial mood before they discussed his children. Rooster listened keenly, frequently scratching his toe. He warned they were running short of time and Bo Aku could get impatient, storm in, and disrupt the meeting.

They all filed outside in a show of solidarity, with Rooster leading the way. They found him on the fence, frowning, with a pile of banana peelings around him. They quickly surrounded him and Spider stepped in front and started speaking in a soft but stern tone.

"Stop! Bo Aku growled. My whole family has disappeared and all you want to do is talk?" He groaned as his eyes grew wider and his forehead wrinkled. Rooster staggered forward scratching his nose with his toe. He told the king the group had organized a concert for him.

Each animal there knew his own role and they were ready to perform. "Wasp would be the drummer, Grasshopper the ballerina, Bee the singer and I the saxophonist," he said, pointing to each of them. He said Spider was better than B.B. King, that Bee was an accomplished artist in country, r&b, reggae, makossa, salsa, blues, and rap. "Last year he won the World Idol contest singing opera," she added. He sang a slow jam song and danced while the rest giggled.

Bo Aku grinned and scratched his jaw with a ripe banana in his hand, wondering whether he should stay and watch the performance. The gesture could also be a sign of fury. He could pounce on them any moment.

"We want to perform for you," Rooster chanted and they started to sing and dance.

"Oh no, not now, I may invite you to my palace later," Bo Aku said. Then his mood changed and he started to talk about his family. He beat his chest and proceeded to give them a a detailed account of what had happened to his family. Bo Aku talked and talked, wiping his sad face with the back of his hand, the banana hanging delicately in the other hand. He said his mother had five children; three boys and two girls. They often spent a full day with no food or water. They shared the little food their captive gave them. He told them a hunter captured his entire family, threw his parents into the river, and handed the children over to a farmer. The farmer's son locked him up in a separate stall from the others because he felt Bo Aku was stubborn and could influence his siblings to fight back. During dreary, lonely days, the young gorilla dreamed about living in a big forest and fetching food on his own.

One evening they heard the farmer's son singing joyfully as he approached and unlocked the barn He pushed the gate and the door opened. Then his family fled into the forest in different directions.

Bo Aku waved his hand to stop a mosquito.

"I have not seen them since that day. I do not know what has happened to them, and I hope that one day I will find them. This is how I ended up here," he concluded, slapping a fly lingering on a fresh wound near his knee.

They nodded and began to understand what had caused Bo Aku's fear and loneliness. Mariel who had been standing behind Mrs. Bella asked him why he had taken revenge on the boys. "They had nothing to do with what happened to you!"

He looked at them, one person at a time, and said, rising to his knees, then to his feet, "The children entered my space without permission. I was concerned they might go back and bring hunters. So I captured them. But your presence here tells me how much you missed them."

"Thank you for understanding," Mariel told Bo Aku, pointing to an area a about a quarter of a mile away from those with pineapples and palm nuts, which the villagers often harvested.

The gorilla arched his neck and glanced at the tree. "Please come out, children!" she shouted.

The children came out, one by one. The Rooster asked them to dance and they obeyed, as Bo Aku smiled broadly.

Bo Aku, pleased to see them again, promised he would never lock up any child, and rewarded everyone with gold, pieces of silver, and a dance of his own. Everyone joined in the dance.

Chapter Four
Rooster Takes on the Lion

On the grass fields and bush farms outstretched along the banks of the Menchum Falls, in the southeast region of the Benue Plateau, lived a brown-skinned lion and his cubs. His name was Botuah, owner of the fields. He roamed the fields from to time, keeping a keen eye on strange creatures. The fields provided a habitat for the grazing and for wild animals. Vipers, pythons, cheetahs, elephants, bears, pandas, gorillas, and other wild animals often came by to visit his family and feed on his leftovers when he was asleep. They considered themselves his friends, but were wary of his temper. They knew he could pounce on any of them and make them his meal. From their own hiding place they had watched him tear up grown up chimpanzees, and tigers whom they revered for their strength. So they always made sure they were out of sight before he woke up.

Cattle owners also known as Fulani herdsmen had migrated from the far northern region near a country called Chad. They had long hair, stood upright and carried a staff and a horn which they used in controlling the animals. They roamed the wilderness for months and sometimes years, seeking green pastures for their cattle. Seen with a small bag strapped to their shoulder, a kettle with water and a staff used to wave off lions and human aggressors, the herdsmen walked among the cattle beckoning the stray ones to stay with rest. Every now and then a mad cow sprinted away from the flock forcing the herdsman to utter familiar sounds to bring it back. *"Aiy-wai, kai-kai"* he shouted. If the cow continued to run wild, he blew his horn and the cow instantly sprinted back and walked forward with the rest.

In the evening, they sojourned in a bush or forest, mostly in a valley or near a river. The herdsmen made a fire, sat in a circle with their feet crossed and discussed their travel plans. Then they prayed, raising their hands toward the sky and looking up. They muttered a few words and washed their face before eating. Then they ate dry bread and drank cow milk while the cows lay nearby moowing and waving off flies from their ears. In the morning, the herdsmen washed their face again with cold water from a stream before they continued the journey southwards. When they found a village with green pastures and nice people they stayed there until the dry season. They wrapped their entire face with a cloth to prevent dust and sand from entering their eyes. They also oiled their bodies with cow milk to reduce dryness and prevent diseases such as atopic dermatitis.

But the goat herders were natives and they knew where to take goats . They were boys aged between five and eighteen. Their family had owned the livestock for generations, so they knew how to tender the animals. They knew when a she goat wanted to mate with a she goat; they knew what to do when a goat was ready to give birth.

The cattle herders and goat herders brought their stock into his habitat to feed on the fresh, lush green shrubs, leaving their dung behind as they chewed away the grassy fields. But they, too, were wary of the unsuspecting presence of Botuah—he could jump out from his hiding place without warning and grab an animal or even a human being with his sharp teeth, drag it away to his slaughter theater, and tear it to pieces before starting to eat. The herder knew the sounds made by a grazing animal and by Botuah and his wife, Natuah. He also knew Botuah was more deadly than Natuah.

Botuah had a luxurious mane that covered the backside of his head, shoulders, his abdomen, and the front of his back legs, and a tassel at the end of his tail, giving him balance. When going for a walk, Natuah would raise her tail, signaling the cubs to follow. She often allowed the two youngest cubs to stay by themselves for the first few weeks in order to bond with their older siblings. She also knew that those youngest ones, born just a few days earlier, were still blind and their eyes would only open in about three weeks, so she relied on her sense of smell to protect them from harm. She had a great sense of smell and could easily smell animals that had been killed by other predators ten to fifteen kilometers away. Then she would rush to the site. Once they saw her approaching, the predators escaped and she feasted until she fell asleep.

If Botuah and Natuah were not hiding in a thicket where they could easily spot their prey without being detected, they were sleeping or touring the wilderness. Each stood three meters tall and weighed almost four hundred pounds, and they strolled around leisurely until they spotted a potential meal. Their countenance turned grave and they chased down the animal and strangled it until it was dead. Then they tore its flesh into pieces and feasted on it. Rodents and rabbits were always unlucky and dreaded them.

Botuah was sneaky and able to get to his prey before being detected. His paws had soft pads and he walked on his toes, which made his movements hard to hear. His forepaws were heavy enough to break a zebra's back and defeat a tiger in a wrestling match. His eyes never glowed in the dark, but he lingered around the farmlands with an immaculate, sandy brown fur coat and shiny pupils hungry for some action. He also knew how to disable the herders or a grazing animal. If Botuah wanted to have more animals for dinner, he would smother the herder before going after the cows or goats that ran wild around the wilderness, confused and terrified. He knew he could easily subdue two or three animals at a time.

The children and their mothers knew he went to sleep in the afternoon after a heavy meal or when it was very hot. They often went in different directions to fetch food or chase down intruders while the cubs ventured into other parts of the grassland. In the mornings and evenings he patrolled the entire fields with his eight children and his wife.

Viper's entire family had been observing Botuah's movements for some weeks. He wanted revenge because they had killed many of his siblings by trampling, but knew his large fangs and deadly venom were no equal for any member of Botuah's family. So he decided he needed help from his own family. He wandered all over the region of Menchum Falls and the neighboring farmlands visiting the Horned Desert Viper, Eyelash Viper, Water Moccasin, Lance-head, Copperhead, Tree Boa, and Pit Viper, holding conferences about his tragedy.

During his last visit Pit Viper widened his fangs and spat on the ground in disgust. "I don't know why we have never thought of this until now," he told an assembly gathered at the bank of the waterfall. "We have holes all across the fields; we have poison, we are very good on grass and in water, slippery, and fast. Are we stooges?" His voice grew louder. "How come we share space with him and his family in this wilderness? We eat what they eat, sleep in the same wilderness, raise our children in the same wilderness, but we have no voice. They have wiped out three generations of our family and all we do is nod our heads and turn the other cheek? Do we want them to destroy all our species and our ancestry?" They glanced at each other and nodded with approval.

"I say we go after Botuah and his family now and bring them to justice, one by one. We must bring them down," cried Tree Boa.

"Wait, just wait a minute, " Lance-Head said softly. "I know I can lie down flat among the weeds and strike any of them without being noticed. But I don't have enough poison to kill."

"Do not underestimate your power. You can do it. Every little bit helps," said Copperhead.

"I know what I can do," Pit Viper said with a deep voice. "You all know I have a heat-sensing blanket in my hole. As soon as I sense the body heat of an animal, I can tell how he looks, and with that knowledge I can bite and poison him. As he drags himself away, dying with my poison in his body, I will follow him and use my heat sensors to track him down and finish the job. Night is the best time for me because the air is cooler outside and the heat of animals is most obvious to me. I can easily detect Botuah and Tiger. Bring them on," he ordered, waving his head.

Desert Horned Viper looked into his eyes and said, "Don't get too excited, brother. Try to kill a rodent first. That would get their attention. If Natuah's baby knows it has been killed, she will investigate the cause because she knows that only they and hunters own rodents here. Be ready to rush into a hole when they come after you."

"But the hole will be too small for her. She is four hundred pounds," Tree Boa warned.

"Then drag the rat's carcass near a lake, to your swamp, anywhere you want. When she comes chasing you, dive into it. She cannot swim. Then just open your fangs and bite her."

"Wishful thinking. Do you really believe lions are stupid? They know they can't swim, so they don't bother to go near a lake," Water Moccasin giggled.

"How do you know they can't swim?" inquired Desert Horned Viper. "You never hang out with them."

"I live here," she said with clenched teeth, pointing to the waterfall with her tail. "In fact, I have lived there all my life and you know that. But you don't visit me—how would you know if anyone else did?"

Pit Viper said in dismay, "If you don't want to help me, I will seek help elsewhere."

"Where else?" asked the Tree Boa. "We have enough arsenals to stop those rude lions. This is our time."

"Stop running your mouth," cried Lance-Head. "You know how to break tree branches and bones, but you have never killed a lion. You are too slow to attack the enemy unless it comes into your den. Your authority is limited to only stupid and unwitting enemies."

Boa jerked his head, "Hey, don't forget you are within my reach right now. If you repeat what you just said, I will break your bones," he warned.

"Listen, guys, I did not come here to start an argument. We have to find a way to slow down the bullies. While you try to figure out a way, I must go outside the family to seek help," Pit Viper said and started to leave.

"Wait. I think Rooster can help. Word is he succeeded in releasing Mrs. Fall's children from the king, Bo Aku," Boa advised.

They were all quiet for a moment, thinking. Then Copperhead said thoughtfully; "Bo Aku may be King of the Forest, but Botuah is the king of this jungle."

"So there are two kings in one land?" Eyelash Viper inquired, blinking with confusion.

"Maybe so, but we can set up a showdown and see who is the strongest."

"Copperhead, you like trouble. If a fight started, would you defend yourself?" doubted Desert Viper.

"We live in this wilderness together, so we can make decisions together," Copperhead replied, gesturing with his head.

"Then go and meet with Rooster," Boa advised.

"He will need to climb up a tree to be in a safe condition to deal with Botuah," Desert Viper advised.

"Will you swallow him?" Pit Viper asked.

"Not this time. As it has been said, we are in this together," Tree Boa agreed.

"Thank you, my dear brothers. You may return to your homes. You will know the result," Pit Viper concluded and left.

When he got home he could not sleep. He rolled over again and again pondering his life in a hole. He felt cut off from the rest of the world. Living in a dark hole was cool, he was protected from the rest of the world and he could strike without detection if anyone invaded his premise. He could easily smell the intruder and attack with his fangs. Since the Botuahs had annihilated most of his family he wanted to make sure the rest of his generation would survive.

One afternoon, he visited the Rooster, shared the sad story, and asked for help.

Rooster asked him to follow him. They went to the Viper, Copperhead, Grashopper, and Bee's residence and Rooster convinced him to have another meeting with Botuah.

They found Botuah in an open ground littered with carcasses, lying under a tree at the far end with his head between his feet. He was just looking around unconcerned. Occasionally his claws reached for his ear to drive away flies and other bugs.

Rooster flew up the topmost branch of the tree under which Botuah was resting and crowed, alerting him. Botuah lifted his torso and glanced around as his ears stood erect. Then Rooster started to speak while Pit Viper kept a keen ear from his hole. Botuah kept his head up.

"We all know you're powerful. You can do anything you want here. Think about it. If you kill all of us, one by one, who will you get to talk to for the rest of your life? Your life will be boring. All of us in this land know you are bigger than us. But we can live together in peace," Rooster said.

"I am bigger than you." Botuah said, tilting his head from left to right and back. He grinned, looking a bit drowsy. "Is that all you can think of? I am a bit thirsty and all you are worried about is my size?"

"Of course we can bring you water if you promise you won't hurt me," Rooster added and promptly skipped to a branch closer to Botuah. He nervously glanced at branches above his head, ready to fly there in case Botuah moved again.

"I have heard that you trick everyone in this forest all the time," Botuah said slowly, rising up to his feet.

Rooster studied his movement and added, "Every problem has a solution. If you do not trust me, I will reach out to my allies. But they may want you to convince them you are trustworthy. They feel you could use force when you become displeased with them."

"I did not hear what you just said," Botuah replied in a deep voice, tottering away from the tree. He then peeked at Rooster to make sure he would not escape.

"I was not trying to flee," assured Rooster. "I want to know what others have to say about this. I will invite them here and you will listen and make a wise decision. Please go back to sleep. Great kings and warriors need quiet time to relax. Enjoy your home, your world."

Botuah leaned against the trunk and soon fell asleep. Rooster toured the forests and grass fields to confer with young, intelligent sources. He met Bee, Spider, Wasp, and Grasshopper, shared Pit Viper's story, and revealed his plans to neutralize Botuah. Bee laughed dryly and asked, "Who in his right mind wants to negotiate anything with a lion? He is the king of the jungle."

"No, we are. Spiders, wasps, and bees can use their strength to change people's minds. Bee can drone and drone all day long, forcing you to pay attention to her," said Wasp.

"Even if I built the largest web in the world, Botuah will still tear it down if he wants. I think we should entertain him first before we discuss what he did to Pit Viper," said Spider.

"When we tell him Rooster worked out a deal with Bo Aku, he might listen." Grasshopper added.

"Great idea," said Bee. "And we must not look nervous when the discussion begins—he might think we are setting him up and retaliate," Spider said.

"Sorry, but he probably knows that and doesn't like the idea. He called me a trouble maker."

"You mean you have already met with the lion? Then why are you here? Why didn't you come here first if we meant anything to you?" Wasp asked angrily.

"Brother, don't sting me, I was simply trying to help someone in need. Now, let us go and have our meeting with him," said Rooster.

"What have we decided to tell him?" Grasshopper inquired.

"Just follow us and go with the flow," Rooster said. They all filed up behind him and scurried toward Botuah's residence in a show of solidarity. Rooster led the way, followed by Grasshopper, Bee, Wasp, and Spider.

They introduced themselves and sat down, facing him. Grasshopper sat near the tree. Then Spider talked to Botuah.

He thought for a moment and said, "That sounds good to me. But what would I get in return?"

"You will be able to come visit us anytime, with no droning, no stinging, nothing," declared Rooster.

"We will organize a concert for you," Spider injected. "I will have a trumpet, Wasp will play the drums and Grasshopper will dance. He is a good dancer too. Bee will sing. He can sing and play any kind of music. Whether you like country, r&b, reggae, makossa, salsa, blues, and rap he will play it for you. Do you want to hear some of it now?"

"I am flattered by your presence here today. You never knew this, but I have always considered you my friends from the beginning of time. You know your place in the jungle and you have made no effort to disturb mine, so we can remain friends. My family and I will continue to live here with you in peace as long as you maintain your space," Botuah said. "You are tiny and you only attack others when attacked."

"We do that to protect ourselves because we are among the smallest creatures in the world," said Wasp.

"I know that. This is why I have never attacked you or used you for food. I know you have to continue to raise your families. You respect your space and that of others. But Pit Viper and his family cannot be trusted; they are sneaky and evil-minded. This is why they hide in a hole all the time. If you put your foot in their hole by accident, they will try to kill you with poison. When they smile and open their fangs, you think they are laughing with you, but all they want is to kill you. They sneak up on you when you're not thinking and attack you when you have done them no wrong. If you step on them by error, they will not forgive you, they will bite you. And they never change. Sorry that I am rambling, but I will not negotiate with evil."

"How can you trust a family that has only tried to keep away intruders? Pit Viper and his family are the soldiers of this land. They kill intruders to protect us," Wasp said in an angry tone.

"They can get hold of an enemy faster than us," said Copperhead.

"You flat headed diabolic reptile, stop talking. You are more dangerous than his family; you strike unsuspecting folk and slip away into the bushes," Botuah complained.

"He's right," Natuah said softly.

"In what way?" Botuah asked, turning sharply toward the serpent. "Those evil vipers kill everything upon sight; they kill with no mercy!"

"They kill only when you interfere with their space. They do not go after those folk who come around their hole without invitation. If you don't tell them you are coming to their hole, why should they welcome you?" Natuah asked.

"I know that," Botuah replied, rising to his feet. He clenched his teeth and frowned, saying, "If it is that you are right, how come all these folk are still here? Grasshopper is here, Tree Viper spoke. The rest of you do not have any bites on your bodies. And Pit Viper is also alive. Even Rooster."

"Do not mention that sleek fellow if you want this meeting to continue," Natuah warned.

"You mean Pit Viper or Rooster?" Grasshopper inquired, trying to show interest in the feud.

"Rooster, of course. Who doesn't know the wily one?" Botuah said.

"My dear husband," Natuah said, leaning forward on her front paws, "you cannot be everywhere at the same time. And you cannot be everything to everybody. You are only one creature."

"I am who I am," Botuah replied, stroking his chest.

"And exactly who are you?" she asked in a rising tone. "Who do you think you are?"

Botuah stared at her. "After the twenty-three years we've been together, you still don't know who I am? Was that a question? Really?"

Natuah shook her head, saying, "Sometimes I wonder whether you are the same one I married."

"Do you mean sometimes or all the time?" Botuah joked.

"These people took the time to come here to see you for you to resolve their problem. If they trusted someone else, they would have gone there," Natuah said emphatically.

"I do not have a problem with these folk. Pit Viper must go!"

"Aha," she replied. "That is why they came here. Sit down and listen to me," she said

"Okay," he said and reluctantly leaned backwards on his paws, with his dewclaw outstretched. "Make it quick. "

"When you are angry, you can't make wise decisions. You want to wipe out a family because you feel they're mean and wicked?"

"Yes of course, look at him, look at his mean, evil face," Botuah said.

"I will remain quiet until you decide to listen to me," Natuah preached, folding her arms in a gesture of resignation.

Botuah breathed loudly before he asked her to continue speaking.

"Since you started killing others because you wanted to feel free and safe, why are you not happy today? Why are you still upset with Pit and his family?"

"Because I have the power to control others," Botuah replied adamantly.

"Power is not a virtue. Life is not always about using force. Words heal. Look at these folks sitting in front of you. They have come to share their thoughts with you so there can be peace."

Botuah dropped his head and thought for a while. "Okay, if they promise me they will make sure those vipers stop killing innocent ones, I will accept their peace terms."

"Peace happens when you give up something and get something back," Natuah told him.

"Is that really the case?"

The visitors exchanged glances.

"You are king here, you should know," she said firmly.

The visitors giggled and waited.

"I may be king, but you've said peace is a good thing. Let's see. I will leave all vipers alone if you promise me they will not kill any other folk again outside their pit."

"You have to also promise these folk that you will not threaten Pit and his family if they continue to protect their own space," Natuah said.

After a moment of silence, he raised his head and looked the visitors one by one, and then he said to them, "No one will be punished as long as everyone maintains order in this land. If any folk enter Pit's residence without the family's permission, Pit will have the right to take any action to protect his space. Go in peace," he concluded.

They thanked him for taking the time to talk to them and left. Botuah returned to his den.

Chapter Five
Children Guard a Farm

Banga, Mani, Bah, Milla, and Beni always worked together and played together. Each had a nickname based on his character. Everyone in the village knew they were the most mischievous children and parents did not want them near their children. Whenever they met, the boys and Beni left behind something memorable. Bah went to the huts where the children lived and beckoned them to follow him. He tottered behind each hut and whistled, and they instantly knew what to do. Then he scurried to the playground to wait for them. It was a rough terrain filled with sharp rocks and dried mud.

Children abandoned their chores and rushed to the playground to meet him. Some left their gourds by the stream to meet their friends, knowing their parents would later punish them for being tardy.

Within minutes, several scores of children had assembled in the playground. They quickly formed a circle around him and listened. Among them were the notorious Beni and Banga.

"We have to spend the night near Bo Aku's place, to develop a friendship with him. If you are scared of him you can leave now," he told them.

No one moved.

"We must remain vigilant when we get there," Banga added, looking directly at each child in the eye.

"We must stay busy," Beni said.

"We will cook and eat his food together," Bah continued.

"And make a mess of his premises," Banga added.

"First, each of us must be aware of his responsibilities. We need a plan," Beni advised.

"Somebody should volunteer to make a fire," Banga ordered.

They looked nervously at each other. None offered to provide the spark with which to make the fire. It was an ordeal rubbing stones to get sparks.

"I will do it," Beni volunteered, raising her hand.

"You?" Banga asked with a cynical look in his face.

"What do you mean by that? 'You?'" she wondered.

"But women do not have the strength to make a fire," he exclaimed, turning to the boys for their approval.

"Hey, hey," replied Beni. "Making a fire is a skill that requires common sense, not brute strength."

"You have no clue who we are," she replied, skipping toward him with her clenched fists above her chest. The boys quickly formed a fence urging her to step back.

"Will you make the fire, then?" Bah asked.

"Wait and see," Beni replied, brushing off her garment.

"Someone must keep an eye at the doorway and everywhere," Bah said.

"I will hide on a tree branch and listen to his footsteps. If I shout once, all of you should flee toward the stream," said Banga.

"Great idea!" Beni screamed

"What? Can everyone here swim?" the shortest child asked.

"It doesn't matter. When danger comes after you, you must fight back, otherwise you die like a fly," Bah advised. "Once you are in the river, swing your arms and legs fast."

"And keep your head above water level the whole time."

"Don't try to swim against the water current. Follow it. You'll be fine."

"Someone in the farm might rescue you."

"Rescue who? What if Bo Aku jumps into the river when you scream?"

"He will drown before you do."

"Oh, he can't swim."

"He's too heavy."

They continued to discuss the details for a few more minutes, and then Bah said, "Are you ready to go?"

"I am," each of them said in turn.

He led the way and they followed.

"Shhh!" Bah hushed them and lifted his finger over his lips. "If he hears us, he will appear in no time," said Bah. "Don't forget he knows every sound in this forest."

"He can scream louder than the lion; he can hop over trees to get wherever he wants. If you are alone, he'll pick you up. We must be careful." Beni interjected.

"I will go fetch a rope and hide behind the door. If he jumps into the hut, I will throw it around his neck and pull it fast enough to bring him down. Then we can jump on him and slow him down," Bah suggested.

The boys quickly grouped together. Standing shoulder to shoulder, they conferred.

"We must devise a ruse to attract him him," Banga said.

"But he is too strong and all of us cannot defeat him," Mani said.

"He gets anything he wants here," Bah said.

"But we have to find a way to do that today. He has ruled this forest for too long. Children cannot play around or hunt freely," Banga retorted.

"He can come here and devour us too," Banga warned.

"Hmm. I have a plan. Let us give him food," Bah said. "I will prepare dinner." He started to make pumpkins and vegetable soup for dinner while the other boys and Beni went away to perform their own tasks and prepare for sneak into Botuah's place.

Mani returned to the hut at dusk with the rope. He was tired and forgot to close the door. He soon fell asleep behind the door with the rope held loosely in his hand.

Darkness arrived. Even the fire flames did not have enough light to help anyone see inside the hut.

Bah heard a voice, followed by footsteps. The lion seemed to be approaching the hut. "Hey! Who is in there?" Botuah shouted.

The children halted. Bah did not answer.

Botuah stopped and called out again.

"Hey!" Bah replied timidly.

Botuah strode in with a swollen, blood-drenched bag strapped to his shoulders and a tambourine in his hand. "Hey, buddy!"

"Hey, buddy!" Bah replied.

"Would you take this heavy bag off my shoulder?" he asked playfully.

Bah hesitated. "Sure," he replied, reaching for the bag as he lowered his shoulder to ease the effort. Bah staggered forward with it and dropped it near the fireplace before he continued cooking the pumpkins.

When it was ready, Botuah asked for the good pumpkins and ordered Bah to eat the tasteless, watery ones.

As he ate, chewing distractedly, the boy watched his jaws, thinking of what to say to entice him. "I have heard you like spicy food," he teased him.

"Of course! How did you know?" Botuah asked, smiling.

"Good word gets around fast," Bah replied.

"Really?"

"Oh yes."

"Me? Are you sure?" he inquired, stroking his chest to make sure.

"Am I sure?" Bah joked. "Do you really mean how sure am I?"

"Everyone in our village likes you."

"Are you sure? But don't they think I'm a bully, someone who only wants certain folk in my area?"

"Don't you bother about them, everybody has a right to their own space."

"Oof, you had me sweating for a while," Botuah replied, breathing a sigh of relief. He continued to eat as the embers slowly faded away.

"Here, try these. They are delicious." The boy offered him the watery ones. He took them. As he ate, the boy retreated to the back of the hut.

From time to time, he flung a hot pumpkin on Botuah's lap and he cried out in pain, looking nervously around and saying, "Wai, wai, wai, who did that?"

"Oh, I am sorry, I didn't mean it," Bah said.

When he became full, Botuah talked to him about his day.

"I went around the neighborhood supervising the forest under the hot sun. I worked all day in my garden, preparing my crops for the rainy season," he said and asked the boy to heat up water for him to shower. The boy put the water pot in the fire, picked up

Botuah's tambourine and began to strike it with his fingers, making up lyrics as he went along:

Some folk think they are very smart until trouble happens to them.
They think they can always succeed if they do not even try.
They go about telling others
I am tough, perhaps foolish, but who says so?
I am here alone, but not alone.
Someone is always watching me who knows everything about me?
Bolo, bolo, bolo, bolo, ling-a-ling ling . . ."

Botuah liked the song so much he jumped out of his chair and started to dance, mocking the boy with his own song:

Oh, play on, my dear fool, play on.
Oh, play on my innocent fool, play on!
Your time is mine now, play on"

He started to feel pain and his facial muscles quickly tightened. When they heard the music, the children dug a hole in the wall with their toes. Bah slapped the tambourine harder, deafening Botuah's ears. When the hole was big enough for their bodies, Banga shouted and the children immediately decoded the message. Bah ran out the door and ordered them to get away. "Otherwise, we will die here when he stops singing," Bah added.

"Dive now!" Beni screamed.

He threw the tambourine in Botuah's face, pushed his body through the hole, and they raced to the village, unaware Banga was not there. He had sprained his knee while dragging his body out of the hole.

The next day, the children went to the bush to fetch dry wood. Banga wandered off into the woods and got lost. The boys searched for him all day to no avail. As dusk approached, they went back to the village.

Botuah and his wife, Natuah, found Banga while returning from a meeting in Bo Aku's residence. Natuah found him sitting on the ground with his back leaning against a tree, grabbed him at once, and dropped him inside her farm bag, for ransom.

They hung the bag on a tree branch and went home. Banga scratched the walls of the bag with his fingers, to escape. Frustrated, he started crying. Botuah hurried back to the tree, lifted him out with one hand, held him close to his face, and said, "If I hear another sound, you will not be found alive!" He widened his eyes and peered into the Banga's frightened eyes

"What is your name?"

"Banga?" the boy coyly replied.

"And what is your family name?"

The boy hesitated, afraid he might go after his family.

"I don't have time for petty games!" he warned.

"Banga Tofu."

"Ah, I know your ancestors. You are from the family of tricksters. We will find out just how clever your people are," he teased, walking off.

He halted, shook his head defiantly, and walked back to the bag. He placed the bag under the tree, lifted the boy, put him next to the bag, and wandered off into the dark forest.

The next morning, Banga's mother went to the village chief and reported her missing son. The chief quickly dispatched a messenger to go throughout the whole village. The man went from house to house beating his gong, telling parents to count their children immediately and report any missing child to the chief.

Bah heard about the chief's action and thought Botuah might have captured Banga. He immediately went looking for the messenger and found him near Mani's home. He shared his experience with Botuah, frantically reenacting the episode. With a stunned but determined look on his face, the messenger assured Bah that the chief would take prompt action against Botuah.

Within minutes, women, men, and children organized themselves into small groups of five and set out to the farmlands and forests, searching for the child. Bah was among them.

There was no reward for recovering him. Parents felt that every child in the village was also a part of their own family.

When they got near the huge, lone hut deep in the forest, Bah waved a hand and they halted. "That is the place!" he whispered.

"Fine. Go in there and act like you are alone," an elderly woman advised.

As he approached the hut, they quickly slipped to the back and took cover. Botuah heard Bah calling out, "Banga, Banga, where are you?"

"I'm in here alone," Botuah replied, mimicking Banga. Bah entered the hut and Botuah jumped out and still reeling from the frustration of the way the boys had tricked him, he ordered Banga to go outside and harvest and cook pumpkins. "When the pumpkins are ready, you will bring them here and serve me. While I am eating, you will contact your people and tell them to bring me twenty pumpkins before I can release you. Understood?" he said. Bah timidly nodded, went outside to fetch the pumpkins. Meanwhile the villagers were tiptoeing toward the tree, looking for him. They found him making a fire and took Banga with them.

Bah looked around for signs of Botuah. When he was sure Botuah wasn't watching him, he dove through a hole.

Chapter Six
Marta Turns Detective on Her Farm

Once upon a time, a woman called Marta owned a chicken and corn farm. She harvested corn, stored it in her farmhouse and returned to her home in the village. When she went back to the farm, she noticed that the corn had disappeared and her chickens had been roasted.

Marta wondered who might be committing such mischief.

Hmm, she thought. *I can find out why this is happening to me.* She poured water on the floor of the farmhouse, closed the door, and left.

The next day, Marta found fresh footprints all over the floor. The footprints did not look like they belonged to children. She had to see who was the culprit, so she returned the next day and made a fire. Then she climbed into the attic with pots full of hot coals and waited.

Soon, she heard people singing and playing drums. To her surprise, the noise grew louder and louder. She peeped through an opening in the ceiling and was shocked. A bunch of happy old men and women with long, gray beards reaching their torsos were dancing toward her farmhouse. The older women had dreadlocks trailing down their knees and toenails; their fingernails were ten inches long. They had their names written in blood-like ink on their clothes; Mr. Toenail, Mr. Rough Claws, Ms Sneaky, Mrs. Glutton, Mrs Hair, Mr Hot Meals, and brother Fast Run.

"I must be very quiet so no one knows I am here," she thought as they approached the front of the hut.

"Lei, lei, we're too clever for them, dim, dim, dim. We are too strong and too clever for anyone," they sang. When they reached the door, the man with long fingers asked, "Who will open the door?"

The rest of the group chorused, "King of the Forest, Bo Aku."

He asked all of the men to help him open the door. They did. "Bo Aku, go up to the attic and bring corn so that we can make corn flour and mix it with hot water and eat the dough with roasted roosters!" Bo Aku asked them to join him, and the men did.

Mr. Toenail asked, "Who will roast the roosters?""

Everyone replied enthusuastically "Brother Fast Run!"

"And who will prepare our dinner," Mrs Glutton asked.

"Brother Fast Run!"they chorused.

"I cannot do it alone, we must do it together," he replied.

Together they roasted five roosters, sliced them up and prepared chicken soup with fresh, hot and spicy herbs. They asked him to taste the food first. He slammed his hand on the corn dough, broke a lump, tore off fleshy slices of chicken, and munched, leaving them only wings and legs to feast on.

When they finished eating, they started *chong*, a special dance for sacred men and sacred occasions in the Kom Kingdom.

Marta poured down a pot of hot coals on their heads.

"Who dropped that fire?" Mrs. Hair asked angrily.

Everyone replied, "Bo Aku's son!"

"It's not me, it is *chong*," he cried.

They continued dancing.

The woman dropped three pots of hot coal at once. Mr. Toenail cried out, "Who did that?"

No one knew. More hot coal fell on their heads and they hustled around the house, screaming in confusion.

Marta poured five more buckets and they ran away, leaving their drums and the rest of the food behind.

She climbed down, smiling with satisfaction, and took their drums to the King's palace, a fenced compound with sixty houses tucked at the foot of Menchum Falls. The houses, each thatched with grass roofs and a single door stood in a circle, ushered by a huge mahogany tree and a tall bulding with door frames bearing carvings of crocodiles and pythons. The building had four staffs from the ground up to the roof. There was a side door facing a small hut where the gods and goddesses of the land lived. Two men clad only in skirts made of dry grass always stood at the doorway with two poisonous spears in their hands. Their faces and torsos bore white stripes. The stone-faced men were guards to the King's palace.

The king praised her and hosted a feast in her honor. As the guests returned to their homes that evening, he ordered his servants to carry leopard-skin clothes and oil and escort her back to her home, showing respect for her great achievement. Any villager who saw them dressed so richly instantly knew they had been blessed by the king.

As they went through neighboring villages, men, women, and children scurried out of their huts and cheered them on. Some gave her hoes, machetes, and other farming tools as gifts. The servants carried them for her.

When they reached her home, neighbors came over to greet her, bringing food and fresh vegetables and wine. They cooked the food and had a feast for days, eating, singing, and dancing.

Chapter Seven
The Greedy King Meets his Fate

A woman lived with her five children in a village. She also owned a farm in the jungle where a huge chimpanzee called Bobam lived. Everyone dreaded him. The wily, strong, and mysterious lion had defeated every animal in the jungle and had made himself king. They had built a palace for him and his entire family in the heartland and they had to worship him every month. They brought him food and wine. Each animal group organized a dance and concert and performed at his palace, while his entire family watched and enjoyed the food. They took instructions from his sons and daughters. Anyone who tried to disobey was quickly arrested and locked away in a barn. His family was not allowed to visit the prisoner.

One day she sent her son to a villager's house about five kilometers away to collect red-hot coals to make a fire. She did not know Bobam had been observing her for some time, looking for the right moment to kidnap her. When the child got to the neighbor's house, Bobam grabbed him and took him to a hole in his palace. There he dumped the boy. The woman waited in vain. She sent another child there. Bobam did the same thing. The woman sent the rest of the children, but none returned. So she decided to go find out what had happened to her children.

Bobam put her in the same hole with her children and covered it with logs. He left his staff near the hole and went to the swamp, his favorite place of entertainment. He placed his hands on his lips and shouted, waving to the animals to come nearer. The lion, elephant, deer, python, gorilla, and their families arrived. Then he summoned them to a clear area and ordered them to organize a festival in his honor and strolled away into the wilderness.

While he was away, some animals heard them crying and stopped by to help. First came the tortoise.

"Please, help us. One day we'll return the favor," they pleaded.

"Who put you there?" the tortoise asked. They told him and he walked away.

The woman heard a rooster crowing and pleaded with him. The Rooster walked toward the bag, unafraid of the red-bottomed Bobam. *Children are the future so a woman's role in the society is priceless*, he thought as he approached the bag. He wondered which living thing in its right mind would imprison them.

Bobam roamed the entire land treating everyone without mercy, but no one ever challenged him. Throughout his life, Rooster had craved a chance to expose Bobam's buffoonery and weaken his authority in the land. This was the right moment and he had no intention to let it slip away.

Standing by the bags, he thought he had a winning plan. He would free those inside. Then he would interview everyone to find the person who could to stand up to Bobam . He went around the jungle looking for the fearless one whose strength and brains could match Bobam in a duel.

No one had Bobam's brute force and towering height, but Bobam lacked speed and the ability to make clever decisions. He thought being slow and steady can win a race, and added tortoise to a short list of animals—Dragon, Wolverine, Tortoise, Hare, and Lion. Tortoise was a good listener and clever. He could find time to plan, but he was too slow and too small—Bobam could easily defeat him. Hare was fast and hyperactive and Lion was strong.

He pulled them to a quiet corner near the river and initiated a discussion to determine the best way to defeat Bobam. They agreed that Lion should face Bobam, but he needed input. Tortoise advised him to listen to everyone before the battle with Bobam. Hare took him to a racetrack and they practiced fast running, and Rooster showed them how he would keep pecking Bobam's red bottom until it bled. Lion worked on tumbling, wrestling, and punching. As they rehearsed, Tortoise went around the trainees and whispered instructions in their ears, and they nodded with approval.

Then Rooster returned to the village and invited everyone to the swamp for a festival he had organized before the children were kidnapped. All small animals had been invited: coackroaches, spiders, tortoises, snails and the rest.

Before it began, Rooster told Bobam he had brought a team to take part in the festival. Bobam, excited by the opportunity to discover what smaller animals had to offer, accepted the request. He waved his hand at the crowd and everyone stopped and listened. Then he announced the entry into the playground of what he called the midgets of the jungle, tortoises. When they appeared on stage, Wolverine and Dragon sneaked and quickly dug a large hole behind the stage.

Hare and Tortoise started dancing gently, swinging their waists and torsos as Rooster played a familiar Zumba tune. Everyone danced, moving their heads and jerking their waists. Bobam sang along with them, jerking his head to the rhythm.

Then Rooster joined in and waved his feathers, clucking at the same time. Hare and Tortoise danced toward Bobam, slowly swaying their arms beckoning him to join the rest in the center of the swamp. The moment he stood, Lion quickly lifted him off his feet and placed his body across his neck. Then he rushed him to the hole, dropped him inside, hurried to the hole where the mother and children were waiting, and took them safely to the village.

And the villagers crowned Rooster as the king of the jungle and the village. Lion was appointed Senior Military Officer; Tortoise Secretary of Intelligence Service, and Hare Sports Minister.

Chapter Eight
Fame and her daughters in the jungle

Mr. and Mrs. Fame and their three daughters owned a small farmhouse in a village called Chubali. One morning she sent her youngest daughter, Jila, to a marketplace. It was five miles away and the only way to get there was trekking. The market was located on a hilltop called Belo. A deep valley with a small stream separated it from the King's palace, but the Fame family did not know that Tohnain, the notorious warlord, lived there. The children had heard rumors of a ten-foot-tall funny man with long hair reaching down to his knees who came out in the evening and sat on the bridge tapping the surface with his fingernails. He allegedly sang ballads aloud all night long, helping mothers to lull their children to sleep.

When Jila approached the valley on the way to the marketplace, Tohnain jumped out, picked her up, put her in a basket and took it into his house under the bridge. Then he went back up and continued singing. Mrs. Fame waited in vain for her return and sent her middle daughter to go fetch Jila, thinking she had lost her way.

The next day she asked her neighbors, but no one offered any useful hints. She sent her oldest daughter. Three days later, none of her children had returned. She and her husband decided to fetch the children.

Tohnain stood up when he saw them sauntering down toward the bridge. He waited until they stepped on the bridge, then grabbed them and placed them in a farmhouse with their children, tied the basket on a tree branch and went away to fetch firewood. Other animals heard them crying and stopped by to help.

First came the Zebra.

"Please, help us," they pleaded.

"But there are no doors there. You can just walk away. How did you get there anyway?" the Zebra asked. They told her and she walked away. Everyone dreaded Tohnain, and they would not dare set his prey free.

Mrs. Fame heard Rooster crowing and pleaded.

Rooster scurried back to the village where he found Banga, Bah, and Milla playing. "There is trouble over there again," he said, pointing in the direction of the farm. "Come here!" he shouted. They assembled in front of him. He set up a scheme to sidetrack Bobam and free the children.

Banga offered to stay up that night and watch Bobam.

"But you are too short to see anything afar," cried Bah.

"My height does not define my skills."

"My size does not define the size of my brain," replied Banga.

"Then let's go for it. They say if you can't win a war, join the warriors."

"We can always try another way to defeat Bobam. Let's try another trick," said Bah.

"I think I have a plan now," said Rooster. "Follow me."

Rooster drifted toward the basket and untied it and they came tumbling out, thanking him and breathing heavily. He picked up pebbles from the riverbed and dropped them in the basket, tied it back on the tree and went off to his farm.

Tohnain returned in the evening very hungry and set a fire under the basket. When the stones started to crack, he thought it was them. "That's their mom," he cheered.

Another explosion went off. "Great, that's her first daughter."

The explosions continued. When the sounds stopped, Tohnain brought down the bag, pulled a calabash of fresh water closer and sat down. Then he opened it.

"What the . . . ?" he cried out in shock, placing his hand over his mouth.

"Who did this?"

He stormed out to the roadside and paced determined to try and imprison anyone found guilty. As each animal approached, he yelled, "Did you untie my basket?"

"I didn't do it," each replied.

The tortoise came along.

"Did you untie my basket?"

"No, but I know who did; it was Rooster," he said. When Bobam saw Rooster returning from the farmhouse with a bunch of firewood on his head, he rushed toward him and asked if he had untied the bag.

"Oh yes, I did," he cried.

Tohnain instead challenged Bo Aku to a duel and they set up a date and time. He asked all the big, heavy animals in the forest to join his camp in the fight while Rooster quietly recruited bees, wasps, and insects.

Rooster jumped up and dragged his hair, trying to grab him with his hands. Frustrated, Tohnain cried out, but the children and their parents danced around, chanting and mocking, "Save your own life!"

"I will return the favor one day," he begged.

They went away and lived happily ever after in their own village.

Chapter Nine
Bo Aku Meets the Villagers

The children had been playing all day when Banga asked some of the boys who were playing nearby, "Do you think it's possible we could make Bo Aku our friend?" Doubt shone on the boys' faces. "He's much bigger than us and we have had many troubles with him since we can remember."

"Yes, this is true, but these are the reasons why we should make him our friend. He wants a family and we have lived in this village with him since we were born. If he wants a family, why not invite him to play with us here in the village and not in the jungle? We'll all be safer playing together here than in the forest where the beasts of the jungle live," said Banga.

"This is true," agreed some of the older boys. The children all agreed to ask their mothers to come to the playground that night, even though some of them didn't think it was the best idea. Once their mothers were there, the children would tell them their idea.

After dinner that night, the children brought their mothers to the playground. Some of the fathers came also out of curiosity to meet him. Old men pushed forward and stood a few meters away from him; children turned back from the river and rushed to the playground. Goat herders tethered their flock on grass nearby and quickly joined the rest. A crowd that had started with just five people soon swelled. Within a half-hour, the whole place was hot and sticky from the heat and the crowd as people chit-chatted with excitement.

"Quiet, please," Bah shouted, waving to the crowd.

Banga said, "We thought of some different ways to deal with Bo Aku and wanted to share them with our parents." Some of the parents were extremely apprehensive just at the mention of the huge ape's name. Bah continued, "We have been captured and let loose from his captivity. We know he wishes to have a family. He lost his real family to hunters years ago and wants to have friends and children around so he won't be so lonesome."

"So what is your idea to stop him?" Banga's mother asked.

"We ask him to come to our village, here at our playground at nightfall after we have all eaten, just like tonight. If he arrives, we will have many of our warriors hidden in the three closest huts. If he attacks we can attack him back with our spears and arrows. We shall have the advantage at night if we have planned it out carefully, but we cannot attack until he shows anger or danger."

The parents' faces showed the look of disdain. "Why allow that huge monster into our village after he has tried to kidnap our children? This is too dangerous and I don't like it!" said Milla's mother.

Banga's father replied to the children, "How did you think of this idea? I do not want to tell you yes or no until I have heard more of your plans. I also do not want Bo Aku to wage war on our village and continue to kidnap our children until none of you are left."

Banga spoke directly to his father in front of the children and parents, "It was my idea, Father. I talked about it to all the children, but when the ones who have been kidnapped by Bo Aku told me what that giant ape wanted, I listen intently. I do not wish for him to be terrorizing our village and I do not want any of my friends kidnapped or hurt."

"True," affirmed Milla's mother. "If we let him come into our village to play with our children, he may do so as long as we can build some mutual trust between the villagers and Bo Aku. We need to work with him to build a friendship so he may be happy with the children here in the village. We could get him to watch over our crops by the river so that we may get a good crop every year, or have him to protect our village from the marauders that come here every year in the spring to attack our village and steal our food."

Marta said, "We must keep those marauders from stealing my livestock and corn. The last time they came I had to climb into the ceiling of my house above the rafters to pour hot coals upon the thieves' heads. I cannot continue to defend myself from those stealing marauders. We could use Bo Aku's help for situations like these."

Banga's father, who was also one of the very best warriors in the village, said, "I will make the arrangements for our village warriors to be placed in the huts in case Bo Aku becomes angry with us for any reason. We will have at least twenty warriors ready to use spears and arrows to chase him back into the jungle if we must. I want no exceptions. These negotiations between our children and Bo Aku must proceed with calm talking and no anger. If he gets angry, he will never provide us with the benefits of protecting our crops, our village, or our children."

The mothers were all worried that their children would be in harm's way should Bo Aku become angry, and they voiced their displeasure at such a plan. Banga's father said, "I shall see if I can get the warriors who are the fathers of these children to hide in the huts. They will make sure that the children won't be harmed. After all, they are the children's fathers."

Milla's mother broke in, "Not only will the fathers who are warriors be there, but so will the mothers. I will not allow my children to stay here alone talking with Bo Aku after dark about an agreement like this! Those proceedings should proceed with parents who can make a reasonable decision about who our children visit and play with!"

Bantu's father had to agree. "You are right. The mothers can sit in a half circle with their children behind them. I will make sure to have three torches set up in the center of the half-circle so that we can all see Bo Aku when he approaches. If he gets angry, all the men can come out of the huts behind the women and children and chase him back into the jungle." He then said to them, "Children, leave the talking to your mothers and only speak when you are asked to speak by your mothers or if Bo Aku asks you something; other than that, you are to be quiet and calm. I don't want to upset that giant ape with so many people around him, especially women and children!"

The next day Banga went to some of the children, asking their opinion on how they would manage to invite Bo Aku to the village for the meeting. Mani and Milla answered, "There would have to be many of us children to invite him there the first time. No one should do it alone, because it won't be safe. With many of us it will be safer. Also, make sure to tell your father we are going to deliver the invitation. He may want to come with us for protection."

When Banga told his father about finding Bo Aku to tell him to come to the village playground, he said, "Banga, this could be very dangerous. I want you to follow directions and don't get hurt! Tell me who the two fastest boys are that you know in the village."

Banga immediately said, "Bah and I are the fastest! We both can blow out the lanterns before bed and be in the bed before the room turns dark."

Banga's father told him, "I will speak to Bah's father to see if he will come with us so you two boys can deliver the invitation, but you must be ready to run quickly if you sense danger from Bo Aku. We must be careful not to anger him."

"Anger him?" inquired Bah, covering his mouth. He did not want them to detect the sneer on his face.

"Why be bashful? Bo Aku can unleash a temper and create trouble with no warning. We must be careful," replied Bah's father.

"Your father and I are both good with spears," Banga's father said. "We are very fast, but I don't want to fight Bo Aku if we can avoid it."

That night Banga's father went to see Bah's parents to discuss the meeting with Bo Aku. Banga was alone in his mother's bedroom. He noticed her beautiful amulet hanging on the wall by a nail. He knew it had been a present from his father to his mother and had taken many months for him to make it out of freshwater pearls and jewels that he gathered out of the creekbanks near the river Ngewi, where he fished. His father gave it to his mother on the day they were married. The jewels shone and glowed red and yellow with the blazing fire in the bedroom.

He removed it and put it in his pocket for the meeting with Bo Aku. He knew that he could be in big trouble for taking it, but he also knew that giving a gift to Bo Aku could signal some trust in the gigantic ape's mind.

After an hour, Banga's father returned and called the boy outside, where he met Bah's father and Bah. They stood there with clasped hands and talked for a long time about the meeting with Bo Aku. They then instructed the boys to run to their father's hiding place in the jungle should the great ape become angered. Banga and Bah strode to a corner and rehearsed every word they were told to say.

That evening, Banga made sure when he was alone before bedtime. He rehearsed words he would use when giving the gift to Bo Aku.

The next afternoon the boys and their fathers met at the outskirts of the village. The fathers came equipped with long spears, short spears, two bows with twelve arrows each, and slingshots with stones for the boys to use if Bo Aku charged. They were leaving nothing to chance with their children in such a dangerous situation.

The two boys walked in front of their fathers in the jungle to meet Bo Aku. After walking four kilometers, they rested under a fig tree and drank the water the men had brought. As they drank, they listened carefully to the raucous sounds in the jungle, keen on picking out any sound of the great ape. The day was hot and the sun shone brightly on the plants and trees. As they were resting, all of them heard noises. "Was that him, father?" Banga asked, looking nervous. His father had told him to expect to be afraid if Bo Aku approached.

He had told both the boys to use wisdom and intelligence to craft the words for the invitation to the giant ape. He warned them not let fear overcome their wisdom and obligation to the children and people in the village.

They walked further into the jungle, aiming to distinguish Bo Aku's footsteps from the birds, waterfalls, squirrels, rodents, hissing snakes and other noises. They heard a noise overhead in the branches of the jungle and looked up.

Banga called out, "Bo Aku, come to us." They only heard a distant noise in the trees from far up the trail. As they continued walking, the noise became slightly louder.

"That could be him," said Bah's father.

"Yes," Banga's father agreed, "we should find our hiding place near here. Boys, proceed thirty or forty paces further up the trail but no further. If you walk you will be out of range of our arrows. We won't be able to protect you that far away."

They agreed, nodding.

"Do you both remember what to say to Bo Aku?"

"Yes," they replied. The boys turned and walked fifteen more paces up the trail, talking to each other.

"Are you frightened?" Banga whispered to Bah.

"Yes, of course!" he whispered back. "Aren't you?"

"I am, I am," Banga said, "but I'm trying to remember the lines that we must deliver to invite Bo Aku to the village playground tonight. Do you remember what to say to him?"

"I do! Don't you remember what you are supposed to say?"

"Not all of it, but I will do my best not to be scared."

"We are supposed to use our intelligence and wit more than our fear!"

Suddenly, they heard a loud noise in the branches in front of them. There was no doubt now. Bo Aku was approaching them from the tree branches ahead. "Bo Aku, come to us." Banga called. He realized his voice trembled slightly from fear, so he repeated his words with a louder and lower voice. *"Bo Aku, come to us!"* Before he delivered the last word, the giant ape's feet hit the ground on the trail a quarter of a kilometer away from them.

They knew from the way the ground trembled when he landed on it. He came warily toward them and with each step Bah became more nervous. Banga warned him. "Be calm, use good sense and not fear," he whispered to Bah.

Banga began with his rehearsed speech. "Bo Aku, the villagers wish to address you tomorrow night just after sundown near the playground at the edge of the village."

"And for what purpose should I come to the village? To be ambushed or killed by your people?" His words seemed to boom through the jungle with great vibrations.

"No, Bo Aku. We wish to discuss mutual benefits with the great master of the trees of the jungle. We wish this meeting to be peaceful and polite," Bah interjected.

Bo Aku shook his head with disbelief.

"None of the villagers wish to harm you," Bah added.

"Peaceful and polite? The villagers have not been peaceful and polite. They have destroyed my family. When I try to build my own family, they do not like it. It has been this way for many years."

"I promise it will be peaceful and polite," said Bah .

"If you come politely and in peace, the villagers will not harm you. I give you my word," Banga added.

"What good is your word? I have never lived in peace with the villagers and I do not trust them." Bo Aku's words penetrated through the jungle as he spoke. Banga and Bah's fathers looked concerned in their hiding place. They began to put the arrows into their bows. Bah's father had also thought to put the boy's slingshots on the ground with the rocks already in them for the boys to use in case Bo Aku charged.

Banga walked two paces forward, reached into his pocket, and lowered his voice. "I have brought you this present. It is my mother's," he said, pulling out the beautiful necklace. "I want you to have it. Keep it."

Bo Aku stared at the shiny amulet. He had never seen anything that pretty and could not believe it was so shiny and colorful. Banga held it out to him and Bo Aku let the boy drop it into his hands "How do I use this?" he asked the boys, holding it above his head.

"It is not for use except as a decoration. It's very pretty but has really has no other use," Banga said.

"I shall be at the village tonight, but you must ensure that I will come to no harm and I will not be forced to fight the men in that village. I will come on peaceful and polite terms, provided I am met with the same."

"Good, we will meet by the playground shortly after sundown and there will be torches to light the meeting place. I will be there also to meet with you and to make sure you are safe and the villagers will be safe," Banga said.

"Very well," said Bo Aku over his shoulder as he walked away from the boys. "Hey!" he yelled before the boys were out of hearing distance. Banga and Bah turned around to face him. "Hey?" cried Bah.

Bo Aku replied, "I don't know your names, do you have names?"

"Yes, I am Bah and his name is Banga," Bah said. "Ask for us tonight and we will introduce you to the other villagers."

Bo Aku was apprehensive, the boys could see it in his face. "Thank you for the pretty string of stones," he said, and with two giant leaps he was in the trees and gone.

Banga and Bah were still frightened when the giant ape was gone from their sight. They realized slowly that they were both staring at the place where they had last seen him and both of them were breathing deeply as though they had been sprinting for a very long time.

Suddenly Bah's father called to them from behind. "Boys, come here if he is gone." The sound of the voice startled them and made them turn around to face their fathers.

"Banga, you boys come here!" Banga's father said. Both boys walked rather quickly toward their fathers, who were standing up with their weapons in their hands. "I'm proud of both of you for doing that. I'm sure you were frightened."

"Yes, we were!" replied Bah. Banga shook his head, reaffirming that he was also quite fearful of being that close to Bo Aku.

"I am happy we did not have to use the weapons we brought with us," Bah's father said. "I think having to use our weapons against that giant beast would have scared me even more. Right now let's head back to the village, and quickly. You can tell us what he said on the way."

Chapter Ten
The Villagers Engage Bo Aku

When word spread through the village that Banga and Bah and their fathers had met Bo Aku in the jungle, everyone immediately thought they were the greatest of warriors and very, very brave. However, when word spread that the four of them had invited Bo Aku to the playground, the villagers became much more cautious of them. They quickly gathered in small groups and chatted nervously. Some confronted Bah and Banga's fathers.

"Are you sure you know what you are doing, putting everyone in the village in jeopardy like that?" Bah's mother asked Bah's father, surrounded by anxious neighbors who had gathered in their kitchen.

"No, I am not sure of the methods to tame Bo Aku, but everyone in the village is tired of Bo Aku's kidnapping our children, laying our farms by the river to waste. This must stop. We have begun measures to work with the ape to stop this behavior from him. We must see what he wants from us and how we can make peace with him."

The mothers in the village knew their part in the plan. They were all to be on the playground at sunset with their children behind them. The three torches were lit and placed between the mothers and the edge of the jungle. The light from the torches lit up the entire playground. Banga and Bah stood behind their mothers in the center. The men had taken their places in the back of the playground, a clearing in the middle of the huts. All of them were armed with spears, bows and arrows, and slingshots. The men kept out of sight so that if Bo Aku became angry and charged, they could spring from hiding to surprise him with their weapons. Everyone in the village hoped that would not be necessary.

After dusk, the villagers heard a slow, steady sound coming through the jungle. It was Bo Aku. The giant ape was approaching. He was slowly heading for the torches. The women told their children to keep still and quiet. Some got behind them. When he appeared barely near the torchlight, the mothers were full of fear.

He was a huge beast! If he became angry and charged, how could the women ever chase their children away from him before he harmed them? Some of the villagers' eyes became as large as saucers when they saw how large this ape was.

That is what Bo Aku saw first. He said, "I see your eyes are frightened. I have come with peace in my pockets. I was told to be polite and you would be polite back to me."

"I am Banga's mother, the boy you met today is my son. We shall be polite to each other. Our children are here with us and we want them to feel safe and out of danger."

"I have not come to hurt anyone, especially your children." Bo Aku spoke deeply and his voice increased in loudness, causing rumblings and vibrations. "What is it you wish to speak to me about?"

Banga and Bah's mothers stood close together now and took a half-step forward but no more. They were too frightened to walk closer to this huge beast. "We want our children to be safe when they are here and in the jungle playing. We do not want to have to come to you when they are kidnapped or lost out in the jungle."

Chapter Eleven
Bo Aku and the Villagers Reach a Deal

Men stood in one corner, women in the other and children in the middle. They were at least three arm lengths from him, safe enough to escape if he suddenly decided to fight. The King and his army were stationed in the back. Bo Aku stood was almost seven feet tall. The two leaders were taller than everyone. The red feathers on both sides of his cap were remarkable whenever he turned his head from side to side to be heard. His garment glittered with gold and mud. It had broad, long sleeves embroidered with python skin. The rest was dyed cloths with trinkets, large diamond rings, and seashells hanging down. Around his neck and wrists were layers of diamond bangles that moved around every time he raised or dropped his hands to adjust his skirt made of zebra skin.

A showdown was imminent. As he approached, they all noticed the necklace he was wearing as it shone amidst the encroaching darkness. Bah's mother looked closer and placed her hand over her mouth in shock.

"That looks like the necklace you gave me as a present," she exclaimed to her husband as more people assembled at the edge of the village.

"That cannot be true. How would the giant ape have had access to it?" Her husband wondered aloud.

Bah fidgeted in a corner with the boys, hoping someone would change the subject. But that did not happen. His mother became angry and wanted to confront Bo Aku.

"It's not a good idea to speak directly to him. You could hurt his ego," Bah's father whispered. "It has taken us a lot of time and various negotiations to bring him here. He could get angry and hurt every one of us."

"But he has my jewel. I must find out how he got it. There is no other jewel in this village like that."

"How do you know that?" he joked.

"Look at his neck. I have spent time around other women. Women know how to keep secrets. If anyone had a necklace designed like that one, they would have been wearing it every day; it is very attractive. You told me you made it just for me."

He glanced at her with a broad smile. The crowd had quickly grown to a sea of heads. Children brandished their bows and arrows. Women stood akimbo with their hoes occupying the space between their legs. Young men had well-sharpened machetes; older men had lined up behind them with knives and spears, all ready for battle.

The crowd kept a close eye on him. Suddenly, Bah's father shouted out to Bo Aku.

The noise vanished.

"I see you have something belonging to my wife. . . ."

"You mean this," the ape said as he slowly lowered his head. He raised his hand and caressed the necklace. Then he moved his head slowly and looked through the crowd.

Bah and Banga had taken cover behind a fig tree a stone's throw away from him. They held their breath as the crowd followed his head movement with their own eyes, curious to see what he would do next.

"Two little ones brought it to me some hours ago. So you have come to take it back?"

"Well, er, no," shouted Banga's father.

"Then why did you ask me that question?"

The crowd became nervous as some looked for empty space to escape.

Bah and Banga dashed into view. "Be calm, be calm everyone!" Banga shouted. Bah drifted near Bo Aku and faced the crowd. Then he made his confession with his head down. He told them he had stolen the necklace from his mother and hoped to use it to befriend Bo Aku.

"How dare you," shouted a woman. "So you steal your mother's most prized possession to give it to a stranger?"

"Wait! He is our friend, he is no longer a stranger here," Banga replied.

"He has lived with some of us over forty years," someone shouted back.

"But he kidnapped our children—how can he be our friend?"

Bo Aku watched and listened as they argued. He tilted his head from side to side to hear what angle the arguments were taking.

"Okay, the boy stole his mother's necklace and stealing is bad. But look at the big picture: he wanted to impress the King of the Forest," said Banga's mother.

"Yes, I think he had peace in mind when he gave away his mother's jewel," Milla's father mentioned. "Bo Aku is wearing the jewel. It is a token of our relationship with him. If he did not like the boys, he would not wear it to this meeting."

Bo Aku nodded in agreement. Then he waved his hand at the crowd and everyone kept quiet. "This is all true, but I do not like those hunters among you. They killed my little ones, how can I trust you?"

As he spoke, the hunters fidgeted among themselves, unsure whether he was referring to them. They had hunted the little apes for food, and now they were standing face to face with their biggest threat.

"There has been more than enough tension among us. We want peace with you," said Bah's father. "We want you to protect our children when they come to your forest. Protect them from the lions and pythons."

"But your chiefs can protect you. They are here with you, as well. Talk to them," Bo Aku told them. He then dropped his hands in frustration and started to walk away, but the boys quickly formed a circle, pleading for him to stay. He halted, turned around and faced the crowd again.

"Please spare us a few minutes and we will get back to you," a man with a cap full of red ostrich feathers pleaded. He was the chief's senior adviser. He blew a whistle with his fingers in his mouth. Hefty men with bare torsos sprang out from various corners to meet him. Their arrows were silent. He then lowered his head and whispered a few words to an old man in a tall armchair—the chief himself. The chief thought for a moment and nodded. He waved a hand at the men to follow him and he led the way, shuffling through the crowd as they snaked their way through, inching closely behind him. He halted in front of Bo Aku and ordered his men to drop their weapons. They did.

"Now step back," he said. They obeyed. He clasped his hands and gave Bo Aku a look of satisfaction. Bo Aku glanced at the heap next to his feet.

"You treat me like I am a bully because I kidnap your children," Bo Aku exclaimed. "Your hunters have tried to eliminate my family. They kill the children and take them away in bags. For some time now I have been roaming the forests almost alone. I have no siblings left. Tell me who the real bully is."

As Bo Aku spoke, Bah's father stroked his beard, thinking of how best to respond without angering the monstrous figure. He knew someone had to speak quickly to disrupt Bo Aku's thoughts. He knew if he did not share his own thoughts that moment, Bo Aku might take their silence for weakness and decide how he wanted the meeting to conclude. He set his eyes on the ape's rough feet to draw confidence before he started to speak.

"You are King of the Forest; you have everything you want. Your life is easy. If the hunters took away your children, I think they just wanted you to feel their pain because you hid their children in that big forest. Were it not for Rooster, they would never find them. You started this problem; you took away our children—"

"Hold it," Bo Aku interrupted. "I kidnapped the children because they were spies. No one comes to my territory without my permission."

"But you have a family, too. You keep talking about your own siblings, your own feelings. But you kidnapped someone's children, too. How do you think their mothers felt? Did you ever warn the farmers before you kidnapped their children?" a woman shouted from the far end. The crowd replied for him, "No."

Silence returned.

Bo Aku moved his feet to the right then to the left. The crowd instantly retreated in fear. The people in the front row started to run in various directions. He waved his hand and rolled his eyes, signaling he was calm.

"Wait!" he ordered. "Somebody asked me a question." They halted. He told them he had been worried the hunters might return and burn his home after they killed his younger siblings. "So I had to retaliate. I could have killed your women one by one. But I let them plant their crops in my forest. I could have mangled the children too. But I let those little ones visit me again."

The village chief waved a hand at the crowd. The space around him cleared and he stood up and arranged his clothes. The people knew he wanted to speak, so all eyes turned to him and everyone stood still. The chief spoke with such calm that it seemed to lull Bo Aku to sleep.

"I appreciate that you have taken time to converse with my people today. I knew that you had the right to retaliate; after all, they were on your turf. This is why we are here today, to understand each other. There are no bullies and no victims. Our people have lived with your family from the beginning of time. Our children go to your place to play, to get to know you better."

"But those boys usurp my peace and scare other animals away when they just show up without telling me," Bo Aku retorted. "I had had enough." He was quiet for a moment. Then he continued, "You think you know me, but you don't."

"We could save you from poisonous, devilish ones," the chief replied.

Bo Aku laughed and pointed behind him.

"My family has lived in that place for centuries too. They lived there with pythons. I strangle the reptiles with one stamp from my foot, and that's it—they die. We don't need help from you now."

"What do you mean?" the chief inquired.

"The other day, I met a man lying on the grass crying. He was alone. He had been gnawed by an elephant. I could see his blood splattered all over the grass. Some blood was still trickling from his chest. I could have walked away. I went down on my knees, grabbed grass and leaves and blocked the bleeding. Then I stitched the spot and took him to my house where he stayed for five days. I took care of his wound before I let him go home."

"You were his miracle," the chief said thankfully. Others nodded in agreement.

"If you need a miracle, be the miracle first," Bo Aku said. " If you want me to be the guardian of your children to protect them from the pythons and elephants when they come to the forest, show me your trust."

"My soldiers dropped their weapons at your feet. That's trust. I will now make a rule to order no more hunting of apes."

"How will you monitor that?"

"I will ban them from hunting in that forest."

"My family roam other forests in the world, too," he said adamantly.

"But you said earlier all your siblings had been captured and killed," someone shouted from the crowd.

"Be quiet," the chief ordered. "When I am speaking, no one else speaks."

Silence returned. He turned back and faced Bo AKu. They argued for a while.

In the end Bo Aku decided he would protect the children whenever they came to the forest. He said he would hunt down any wild animal who dared to touch them and lead them out of the forest if they were confronted with any other kind of danger.

The chief promised no one would hurt any of Bo Aku's family members in other forests, and ordered everyone to leave.

The crowd dispersed. With two leaps, Bo Aku was out of sight.

About the Author

Emmanuel K. Ngwainmbi is the author of twelve books, numerous articles, book chapters, white papers, and monographs on black experiences, Africa's development, international communication, and globalization. His writings appear in academic and trade publications such as the Columbia University International Affairs online journal, University Press of America, Sage, Lynne Reiner, Rutledge, and Greenwood Press. Prof. Emmanuel has also contributed to a number of anthologies including the *Encyclopedia of African Religions and the Handbook of Black Studies*. He has been Director of International Education Programs and Department Head in a number of universities and colleges. He has held senior positions in other organizations, and lectures widely in the US, Germany, Sweden, Norway Asia and Africa on the confluence and impact of globalization on indigenous communities. He has been a commentator on *Voice of America* radio; BBC-Africa; West Africa Democracy Radio, and other cable television stations in the US, Europe and Africa.

He serves as a senior communication consultant to various United Nations and intergovernmental agencies, and is on the Editorial Board of peer-reviewed journals the likes of Intercultural Disciplines (JID), Development and Communication Studies, and Literature & Art Studies. He is a member of various national and international communication and literary organizations such as the International Association of Intercultural Communication Studies, Poets & Writers, the Academy of American Poets, and the American Society of Journalists and Authors. A recipient of a number of awards including the Distinguished Professor Award from The Chinese Academy for Social Sciences, he reviews articles and books for various professional journals.

His next novel, *Leap in the Dark,* is scheduled to be released by Koehler Books in Spring, 2015.

Curious about other Crossroad Press books?
Stop by our site:
http://store.crossroadpress.com
We offer quality writing
in digital, audio, and print formats.

Enter the code FIRSTBOOK
to get 20% off your first order from our store!
Stop by today!

Lightning Source UK Ltd.
Milton Keynes UK
UKHW051917300622
405194UK00001B/3